Goat Pie

Collect all books in the
Troll Trouble series

Trolls Go Home!
Trolls United!
Trolls on Hols

Goat Pie

by Alan MacDonald

illustrations by Mark Beech

BLOOMSBURY

PRIDDLES: Roger, Jackie and Warren
Description: 'Pasty-faced peeples'
Likes: Peace and quiet
Dislikes: Trolls

MR TROLL: Egbert / Eggy
Description : Tall, dark and scaresome
Likes: Roaring, tromping, hiding under bridges.

MRS TROLL: Nora
Description: Gorgeous (ask Mr Troll)
Likes: Huggles and kisses, caves, the dark

ULRIK TROLL
Description: Big for his age
Likes: Smells, singing, Rockball.

GOAT
Description: Strong-smelling, beardy beast
Likes: Mountains, grass
Dislikes: Being eaten

For Jo, Tim, Joss, Louis and Ellis – A. M.
To my good friend Brandon Buth – M. B.

First published in Great Britain in 2007 by Bloomsbury Publishing Plc
36 Soho Square, London, WID 3QY

Text copyright © Alan MacDonald 2007
Illustrations copyright © Mark Beech 2007
The moral rights of the author and illustrator have been asserted

A CIP catalogue record of this book is available from the British Library

ISBN 9780747586296

All papers used by Bloomsbury Publishing are natural, recyclable
products made from wood grown in well-managed forests.
The manufacturing processes conform to the environmental
regulations of the country of origin.

Printed in Great Britain by Clays Ltd, St Ives Plc

1 3 5 7 9 10 8 6 4 2

www.bloomsbury.com/trolls

Love and Huggles

ULRIK SAT DOWN at the table and cleaned out his ear with the end of his pencil. All week his mum had been reminding him to write a thank-you letter to his grumpa. He began in his big scrawly handwriting . . .

Dear Grumpa,

Thank you for my goatskin hat. It is uggsome! The flaps keep my earses warm.

I wear it when I go to school and also in bed. Dad says it is a hunting hat so next time we go hunting I'm going to wear it.

He sucked the end of his pencil, which tasted of earwax. It looked like the yellow bits of boiled eggs but had a different flavour. When would his dad actually take him on his first goat-hunting trip? he wondered. Since they had left the far blue mountains of Norway, Ulrik hadn't seen many goats. There were none on Biddlesden High Street or in the park along the road where only the fat ducks bobbed on the lake. He turned back to his letter.

We live in a nice cave here. It is called Number 10. It has got lots of rooms. I've got my own. I have done a mud picture on the walls and it is me and Mum and Dad and you outside our buggly old cave in the mountains.

Mum says my roar is getting more scaresome. If you heard it, Grumpa, you would have to cover your earses. I do roaring and tromping practice with Dad every morning on the big hill in our back garden. Sometimes our next-door nibbler puts his head out the window and roars back at us, but I don't think he's very good at it yet.

That's all I can think of right now.

Love and huggles
Ulrik x
PS (That means pssst! there's more)
What are you doing for Trollmas this year? Are you coming to stay?

Ulrik folded up the letter and put it in an envelope – he could post it in the big red letter-hole on the way to school. That was what you did with letters. He wondered how his letter could travel all the way to the far blue mountains of Norway. It must be a long way for the post peeples to walk.

After school Ulrik sat down to supper with his mum and dad. Mrs Troll placed three plates in front of them, looking pleased with herself.

'What's this, Mum?' asked Ulrik, sniffing the two orange lumps on his plate.

'Fish's fingers,' said Mrs Troll. 'I thought we'd try something new.'

'Fish don't have fingers,' said Ulrik.

'Of course they do, my ugglesome. The fingers are the best bit.'

Mr Troll wrinkled his snout in disgust. 'I'm not eating fish!'

'Try it, Eggy. It might be tastesome,' said Mrs Troll.

'Huh!' grunted Mr Troll. He picked up a fish finger and examined it as if it was a nasty insect. Gingerly he bit off the end and chewed it for a moment.

'*Pleugh!*' A half-chewed fish finger landed on the table. Mrs Troll sighed and put it on her own plate. It was the same every time she brought home something new.

'I don't mind the fingers, Mum,' said Ulrik.

'Thank you, hairling. So tomorrow is your last day at school?'

'Yes, not long to Trollmas now,' said Ulrik, his eyes shining. 'What are we having for dinner on Trollmas Day?'

'Goat pie,' said Mr Troll. 'We always have goat pie at Trollmas*.'

Mrs Troll gave him a look. 'And where for uggness sake are we going to find it? I've tried every shop in Biddlesden.'

'We'll find it,' said Mr Troll confidently. 'You can't have Trollmas without goat pie – it wouldn't be the same.'

Mrs Troll put down her knife and fork. 'Well, it *can't* be the same, can it, Eggy? I mean, not like it is at home.'

'Bogles to that! We're going to have the best Trollmas ever, aren't we?' said Mr Troll with a wink at Ulrik.

---

* *Trollmas – Like Christmas, this falls on 25th December. Trolls like the dark and at Trollmas they celebrate the dark days of winter going on and on and on.*

'Yes, Dad!' said Ulrik. 'Can we go roaring*?'

'Of course we'll go roaring,' said Mr Troll. 'We can start next door.'

Mrs Troll frowned. 'At the Priddles'? Is that a good idea? You know what peeples are like – they get frighted if you sneeze at them.'

Mr Troll waved this aside. 'I want us to have a proper Trollmas,' he said. 'Goat pie, presents and lots of roaring. We're not going to change things just because we're not at home.'

'You sound just like Grumpa,' said Mrs Troll. 'That reminds me, Ulrik, have you written your thank-you letter?'

'Yes, I wrote a whole page,' answered Ulrik proudly. 'I wonder if he will come for Trollmas.'

Ulrik's parents stared at him open-mouthed. 'Grumpa?' said Mrs Troll. 'Come here?'

'Yes, we always see him at Trollmas,' said Ulrik. 'I asked if he was coming.'

---

* *It is a troll custom to go roaring from cave to cave on Trollmas Eve. Going roaring is similar to carol singing but less tuneful. Neighbours often throw rocks at the roarers to show their appreciation.*

Mr Troll groaned and hid his face in his hands.

'Ulrik, hairling, try to remember,' said Mrs Troll. 'What exactly did you write in your letter?'

Ulrik tried hard to think. He didn't know what he'd done wrong but judging from his parents' faces, it was something pretty bad. 'I just said something like: "Are you coming for Trollmas?"'

Mr Troll's head thumped on the table.

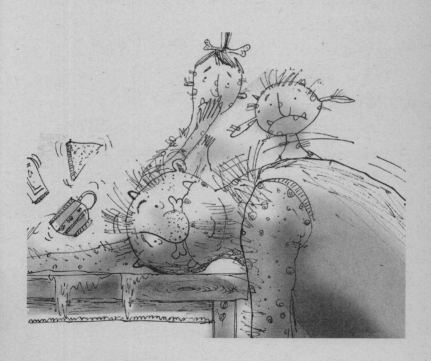

'Maybe he won't come,' said Mrs Troll hopefully.

'Why?' said Ulrik. 'Why can't he come? He always comes for Trollmas.'

'But that was at home, hairling!' explained Mrs Troll. 'At home we lived in our stinksome cave. Things are different here. Grumpa wouldn't like it.'

'Why wouldn't he?' persisted Ulrik.

Mr Troll raised his head. 'Grumpa's old. You know what he's like, Ulrik. He believes in the old trollish ways. He could never get used to living with peeples.'

'Besides,' said Mrs Troll, 'he'd get a bit of a shock.'

'Why?' said Mr Troll.

Mrs Troll looked uncomfortable. 'Well, he might have got a bit muddled. There were a few things I put in my letters . . .'

Mr Troll frowned. 'What sort of things?'

'Just normal things. That we live in a cave. That the neighbours are trolls. I might have mentioned we go hunting in the forest every day.'

'The forest?' Mr Troll roared. 'There is no blunking forest!'

'You've been telling Grumpa fibwoppers!' said Ulrik, shocked.

'Only tiddly ones,' said Mrs Troll.

'They sound hulking big ones to me!' observed Mr Troll. 'Why for uggness' sake didn't you tell him the truth?'

Mrs Troll rubbed her snout. 'I don't know – it just seemed easier! From his letters he obviously thinks Mountain View is in the mountains and all our neighbours must be trolls. I didn't want to upset him. Not after the way we had to leave . . .'

Ulrik shot an anxious glance at his dad. The reason they left home was a forbidden subject. His dad had been butted off a bridge by a charging billy goat. It was because of the bridge trouble that they couldn't go home. Dad said all the other trolls would be laughing behind their backs.

For a moment no one spoke. They all sat round the table staring at the cold fish's fingers and thinking what a shock Grumpa would get if he ever came to visit. Suddenly Mr Troll sprang to his feet. 'The letter!' he shouted. 'Ulrik, what did you do with it?'

'I put it in the letter-hole,' replied Ulrik.

'When? When was this?'

'This morning on the way to school.'

'Then maybe it's still there!' said Mr Troll. 'We could get it back before it goes to Grumpa!'

'Yes!' Mrs Troll had leapt to her feet too. If the letter didn't reach Grumpa he wouldn't get Ulrik's invitation and he wouldn't come for Trollmas. They were saved!

'Come on, Ulrik!' said Mr Troll, grabbing his son by the arm. 'Show me!'

A Tight Fit

THE RED POSTBOX was on the corner of the road in front of the old church. Ulrik peered through the dark slot that looked like a yawning mouth.

'Can you see it?' asked Mr Troll.

'I can see some letters,' said Ulrik. 'There's hundreds of them.'

'But can you see *yours*?'

'I don't know. They all look the same!'

'Here! Let me look!' said Mr Troll, impatiently. Ulrik moved aside to let his dad peer through the hole. He watched as he squeezed his hand through the narrow gap and tried to wriggle the rest of his arm through. It looked very odd, as if the letter-hole was trying to eat him a bit at a time.

'What if someone comes, Dad?' worried Ulrik. He wasn't sure you were allowed to fish around in letter-holes.

'Shh!' said Mr Troll. 'I've almost reached one . . . Got it!'

'Is it mine?'

'Wait a minute – I can't see it yet.'

Mr Troll tried to extract his hand. It had been a tight fit forcing his brawny arm through the hole, but getting it out proved harder still. He pulled and tugged. He faced one way and then the other. He wedged both feet against the bottom of the postbox and heaved as if it was a tug of war.

'GNNNNHH!'

'What's the matter, Dad?' asked Ulrik.

'What does it look like?' roared Mr Troll. 'I'm STUCK!'

Ulrik took hold of his dad's free hand to try and pull him free. They were so busy heaving and

tugging that they didn't notice a red post van turn the corner and draw up beside them. The postman climbed out. He approached rather nervously when he saw the two trolls – the small one and the big ugly one who seemed to be trying to climb inside the postbox. He left his keys in the ignition in case he needed to drive off quickly.

'I don't want to interrupt but I need to get in there,' he said.

'You won't do it,' Mr Troll replied. 'The hole's too small.'

'No.' The postman held up a bunch of keys and shook them. 'I mean I need to unlock it. You'll have to move.'

'How can I?' said Mr Troll. 'My arm's stuck!'

'We were trying to get a letter,' explained Ulrik.

'Were you?' said the postman, feeling a little less nervous now. 'It's against the law, you know, stealing letters.'

Ulrik looked alarmed. 'Oh no, we weren't stealing,' he said. 'It's my letter. I posted it but now I want it back or else my Grumpa will come for Trollmas and he thinks there are goats in the forest.' This came out in one breath and a bit muddled so that when the postman replied, 'I see,' it was plain from the look on his face that he didn't.

'Move to one side, then,' said the postman. Mr

Troll shuffled out of the way as best he could with one arm jammed in the postbox. Ulrik squatted down to watch as the postman unlocked a door and began to scoop the letters and parcels into his sack.

'All right,' he said, seeing Ulrik's anxious face. 'I shouldn't ask this, but which one is yours?'

Ulrik gazed at the sack full to the brim with letters. 'I don't know. It had a stamp on it – a lady in a funny hat.'

'That'll be the Queen,' smiled the postman. 'She's on all the stamps.'

'Hurry up!' moaned Mr Troll. 'My arm's going to drop off!'

'Anything else?' the postman asked Ulrik. 'When did you post it?'

'This morning,' replied Ulrik.

'Oh well, I'm afraid you're too late then. It'll have gone in the first post!'

'Gone?' repeated Ulrik.

'GONE?' cried Mr Troll in despair.

'That's right. It'll be at the sorting office by now.'

The postman tightened the neck of his sack and slammed the door of the postbox shut.

'ARGHHHHHH!' roared Mr Troll, falling backwards.

'Look, Dad,' said Ulrik. 'Your arm's come unstuck!'

For the next week the Trolls checked the post every day. They clung to the slim hope that Ulrik's letter might not have reached Troll Mountain. But on the following Saturday, a tatty, dog-eared envelope tumbled through the letter box.

'It's from Grumpa!' cried Ulrik, hurrying in to show his mum and dad. He tore it open and read out the few words scrawled on the grubby piece of paper.

Dear Ulrik,
Thanks for inviting me for Trollmas. Will arrive Sunday.
Yours roaringly,
Grumpa

Mrs Troll closed her eyes. Mr Troll thumped his fist on the table, making the bowls and plates jump.

'When's Sunday?' asked Ulrik.

'Tomorrow,' said Mrs Troll. 'Surely he can't mean tomorrow?'

Mr Troll slumped back in his chair. 'We're done for,' he groaned. 'We're up the creek without a puddle.'

'I'm glad Grumpa's coming,' said Ulrik. 'I miss him.'

'But what are we going to do?' asked Mrs Troll. 'What about the forest and the goats he'll be expecting?'

'We'll just have to keep him indoors,' said Mr Troll.

'For the whole of Trollmas? And anyway where's he going to sleep – in our room?'

'Not on your bogles!' said Mr Troll flatly. 'He snores like a warthog!'

'Then he'll have to go in Ulrik's room,' said Mrs Troll.

'Where will I sleep?' asked Ulrik.

'In with us, my ugglesome,' replied Mrs Troll.

Ulrik didn't mind that for a few days. It would be just like being home in their old cave where they all huddled together for warmth.

Mrs Troll glanced around the room. There was so much to do and so little time before Grumpa arrived. She would have to go through the house, dirtying the place from top to bottom. Grumpa would be expecting a dark, draughty cave with cobwebs and mouldy leaves. Recently she'd noticed the house had started to lose its smell. The TV would have to be packed away out of sight, so would Ulrik's bed (Grumpa would expect to sleep on the floor in the dirt).

'Ulrik,' she said, 'see if you can find some bugs and spiders for your room.'

'OK, Mum.'

'And Eggy, this house hardly smells. We'll need some fresh cow-patties.'

'What about next door?' said Mr Troll.

'You won't find any there!'

'No!' said Mr Troll. 'I mean, what about the Priddles? You told Grumpa we live next door to a nice family of trolls. What's he going to say when he finds out the neighbours are peeples?'

Mrs Troll put a hand to her mouth. 'Good goblins! I'd forgotten that.'

'Maybe he'll like them,' said Ulrik. 'I like peeples. They can't help being ugly.'

Mr Troll shook his head. 'Grumpa will go tromping blunkers! You know how he feels about peeples!'

'Then we'll have to make sure he never sees them,' said Mrs Troll.

Mr Troll rolled his eyes. 'And how the bogles are we going to do that?'

At Number 8 the Priddle family were also sitting down to breakfast. Mrs Priddle poured some muesli into a bowl while her plump, freckled son, Warren, spread a mound of peanut butter on his third slice of toast. Mr Priddle opened his newspaper, hoping for a few minutes to read it in peace.

'Roger!' said his wife. 'When are we going to talk about Christmas?'

'Mmm,' mumbled Mr Priddle.

'Are you listening to me?' said Mrs Priddle. 'You know the Snorleys are coming?'

'Mmm,' repeated Mr Priddle. He lowered his newspaper slowly. 'The Snorleys? Why on earth did you ask them?'

'Mum!' protested Warren.

'Don't talk with your mouth full, Warren,' said Mrs Priddle. 'Of course I invited the Snorleys. They had us last year.'

'Yes, and it was a disaster. I thought I was going to die of boredom!' said Mr Priddle.

'Don't exaggerate,' said Mrs Priddle, reaching for her cup of tea.

'I'm not exaggerating. Brian Snorley showed us his photos. For two hours!'

'Well, it's nice he's got a hobby. I wish you had one.'

'Jackie – they were photos of train stations!'

'All right, I admit the Snorleys may not be very exciting but it's our turn to have them.'

Warren swallowed his toast. 'Well, I'm not coming,' he announced. 'If we've got to see the Snorleys, I'm not coming.'

'Don't be silly, Warren,' snapped his mother. 'It's at our house – how can you not come?'

'I'll stay in my room,' scowled Warren.

'It's Christmas Day. I expect you to behave nicely and play with Alice.'

'Alice Snorley?' snorted Warren. 'She's weird. She only eats vegetables.'

Mr Priddle sided with Warren. 'I'm not spending Christmas with the Snorleys either and that's flat,' he said.

'I've invited them!' said Mrs Priddle. 'What do you want me to say? "Sorry you can't come, my husband finds you boring?"'

'Well, at least invite someone else!' said Mr Priddle.

'Who?' asked Mrs Priddle. 'The Hoopers are going skiing, the Johnsons are away, we're not even speaking to the Butterworths.'

Mr Priddle racked his brains. There had to be someone else. Someone more fun than the Snorleys. Someone who would make Christmas Day go with a swing. A wild, reckless thought occurred to him.

'I suppose there's always the Trolls,' he said.

His wife gave him a withering look. 'That's one of your jokes, is it?'

'They are our neighbours. They've had us to supper but we've never actually invited them here.' Mr Priddle was starting to warm to the idea.

'You don't have to invite them,' said Mrs Priddle. 'They just turn up at the door. Dragging in mud on their great clumsy feet, smelling of earth and sweat and heaven knows what. Last time Mr Troll licked my hand. *Licked* it!'

'Maybe he wanted to see what you taste like,' said Warren.

'But you can't say they're boring,' argued Mr Priddle.

Mrs Priddle was about to say a good many things but just then the doorbell rang.

'Good gravy! It's them!' hissed Mr Priddle, going into the hall. Three dark shadows could be seen through the dimpled glass of the front door. 'You don't think they heard us talking?'

'Don't be silly, Roger,' said Mrs Priddle. 'See what they want.'

Mr Priddle opened the door and took a step back at the sight of the three smiling trolls outside. Mrs Troll was wearing her best dress – the one with the ra-ra skirt that showed off her thick, hairy legs.

'Hello, Piddle,' said Mr Troll. He imprisoned Mr Priddle in a mighty hug that lifted him off his feet. Mrs Priddle hid behind Warren. The trolls walked straight into the lounge, where they squashed on to the sofa and made themselves comfortable.

'We've got a tiddly problem,' began Mr Troll. He looked at his wife, unsure how to go on. Mrs Troll took over. 'It's Eggy's dad – we call him Grumpa. He's coming to stay with us for Trollmas.'

'You mean Christmas,' corrected Mrs Priddle.

Mrs Troll shook her head. 'No. Peeples have Christmas, trolls have Trollmas. We all sit in the dark and roar at the Great Troll in the sky.'

'Sounds fun,' said Mrs Priddle, thinking it sounded completely batty. 'So what's the problem?'

Mrs Troll hesitated.

'Grumpa thinks that you're trolls,' said Ulrik.

The Priddles stared at them. 'He thinks *we* are trolls?' repeated Mrs Priddle.

'Yes. He's old. He gets a tiddly bit muddled,' smiled Mrs Troll.

'And Mum wrote it in her letters – that you're trolls,' explained Ulrik, helpfully.

Mrs Troll was starting to wish she'd come by herself. Egbert was being no help at all. He had plucked a banana from the fruit bowl and was sniffing it.

'Well,' said Mr Priddle, chuckling indulgently. 'I can't say anyone's ever mistaken me for a troll before.'

'No,' agreed Mr Troll. 'You're as baldy as a bottom.'

Ulrik frowned. 'Your bottom isn't bald, Dad. It's hairy.'

'Yes, but peeples have baldy bottoms, don't they, Mrs Piddle?'

Mrs Priddle felt the conversation was getting off track. She really didn't wish to compare bottoms with her neighbours on a Saturday morning.

'Anyway,' she said, 'I don't really see the problem. Your father will see for himself that we're not trolls.'

Mrs Troll looked awkward again. 'That's the troubles – we *want* him to think you're trolls. He hates the sight of peeples. So we wondered if you could keep out of sight for a while?'

'Keep out of sight?' repeated Mrs Priddle.

Mr Troll nodded. 'Stay in the house. Just until Trollmas is over.'

Mrs Priddle exchanged looks with her husband. 'You're asking us to hide indoors for the whole of Christmas?'

'Exactly!' said Mrs Troll. 'If you don't mind.'

'Oh, why should we mind?' said Mr Priddle. 'It's only Christmas. We'll turn off all the lights, shall we, and creep around in the dark?'

'Good idea!' said Mr Troll.

'Or, better still, we could stamp around the house and roar like trolls.'

'Uggsome!' said Mr Troll. 'But you'll need lessons. Your roaring wouldn't fright an earwig.'

There didn't seem to be any more to say.

He stood up with the banana still in his hand. Mrs Priddle snatched it back off him.

'I've never been so insulted!' she fumed.

'Haven't you?' said Mr Troll.

'Never! You come round here wanting us to hide away as if we're . . . criminals. The nerve of it!'

Mr Troll's face fell. 'So you won't?'

'NO!'

'What about keeping the curtains closed?'

The Trolls left, driven out by Mrs Priddle who aimed a banana at Mr Troll's head as they hurried down the drive. She slammed the door shut behind them and turned on her husband.

'And you wanted to ask them for Christmas!'

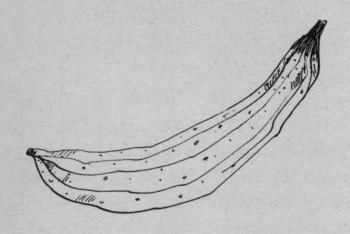

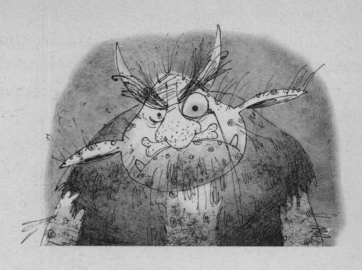

Grumpa

SUNDAY ARRIVED. Mr and Mrs Troll were in a state of nervous anxiety. Would Grumpa really come? It was a long journey from the mountains of Norway. As the day wore on they began to hope that he might have changed his mind.

By seven o' clock only Ulrik hadn't given up and kept watch from the window. Despite his parents' misgivings, he was looking forward to seeing his grumpa. He had already started to think of presents he could buy him for Trollmas.

Goat skulls were Grumpa's real favourite – he had an impressive collection hanging on the walls of his cave, although . . .

Just then a taxicab turned into Mountain View and pulled up outside the house. As the door opened, Ulrik heard a familiar deep, growling voice. Grumpa got out wearing his ancient goatskin coat. He seemed to be having an argument with the taxi driver.

Eventually the driver tossed his bag out on to the pavement and drove off at high speed with a squeal of tyres. Ulrik ran downstairs, calling to his mum and dad, 'He's here! Grumpa's here!'

They hurried out to meet him at the gate. 'Hello, Grumpa!' said Ulrik, hugging him. Mr Troll and Grumpa roared in each other's faces and thumped one another on the back.

'Have a good trip?' asked Mrs Troll.

'Do I look like I've had a good trip?' growled Grumpa.

'Well . . .'

'It nearly killed me. Nothing but peeples since I left home. Peeples on boats, peeples in motor cars. The smell of them! I was nearly sick. Where are all the trolls?'

'Come in! Let me take your bag,' said Mrs Troll, quickly changing the subject. Grumpa stepped through the door, still grumbling about the taxi driver who had demanded money from him.

He looked around. 'Funny looking cave,' he sniffed. 'Doesn't smell right.'

'It's got an upstairs, Grumpa,' said Ulrik. 'You're sleeping in my room!'

'Why don't you show him, my ugglesome?' suggested Mrs Troll.

Ulrik bounded up the stairs, carrying Grumpa's bag.

'I helped Mum dirty my room for you,' he said, pushing open the door.

Ulrik's bed had been removed so that the room was bare except for the mud and leaves covering the carpet. On the window stood Ulrik's rock collection and one wall displayed his mud painting of home. Grumpa surveyed the room. 'Humph!' he said. 'It'll do, I suppose.'

'Look, Grumpa, you can make it dark!' said Ulrik. He flicked the light switch on and off.

Grumpa went to the window and looked out over the neat, lawned gardens of Mountain View. Luckily the Priddles were all in their house, safely out of sight.

'Where are the mountains?' said Grumpa.

'Oh, there aren't really mountains,' said Ulrik.

'No mountains?' said Grumpa. 'I've lived in mountains all my life.'

'We've got a hill,' Ulrik said, pointing it out. 'Dad made it all by himself.'

He pointed to the mound that took up most of the back garden.

'Call that a hill?' snorted Grumpa. 'It's not even a pimple!'

Half an hour later they sat down to supper. Mrs Troll had spent hours at the supermarket trying to choose something that Grumpa would like. She dropped a smoking black lump on to his plate. Grumpa prodded it with a finger.

'What's this?'

'Beefboogers. It's a bit like goat. Try it,' urged Mrs Troll.

Grumpa sniffed the meat, which had got slightly burnt when it caught fire.

'Don't you think Ulrik's grown?' asked Mrs Troll, trying to distract him. 'Stand up, Ulrik. Let Grumpa look at you.'

'Mu-um!' protested Ulrik. He stood awkwardly while Grumpa looked him up and down.

'Looks a bit scrawny to me. Have you been feeding him?'

'Oh yes,' said Mrs Troll. 'Most nights we have fresh goat, don't we, hairling?'

'Um . . . goat, yes,' said Ulrik.

'That's right,' said Mr Troll. 'I've eaten so many goat pies sometimes I think I'll turn into one. Ha ha!'

Ulrik blinked at his parents. He hadn't tasted goat since they'd left home. It was odd – his parents were always warning him to tell the truth but here they were telling Grumpa the most enormous fibwoppers and expecting him to back them up.

Grumpa was asking him a question – something about his hunting hat.

'Oh, it's in my school bag,' replied Ulrik.

'Wear it to go hunting, do you?' asked Grumpa.

Ulrik glanced uncertainly at his dad, who nodded urgently.

'Um, yes . . . I wear it a lot,' said Ulrik.

'And how many goats have you baggsed so far? By yourself, I mean. Four? Five?'

Again Ulrik looked at his dad, who held up ten fingers behind Grumpa's head.

'Well, none yet . . .' he said truthfully.

'NONE?' roared Grumpa.

'Not yet, Grumpa.' (Mr Troll hid his face in his hands.)

'Know how many goatses I'd baggsed when I was your age?' asked Grumpa.

Ulrik shook his head.

'Sixteen,' said Grumpa. 'Six-teen.'

'Uggsome!' said Ulrik.

'And I dragged them home by myselves, miles through that forest and up to Troll Mountain. The snow was so cold . . .'

'. . . it froze your toeses,' completed Mr Troll

wearily. 'We know. You've told us before, Dad.'

'Well, and what is Ulrik learning here?' demanded Grumpa. 'In a place with no mountains and a cave that's hardly got any stink?'

'I've learned lots at school, Grumpa,' said Ulrik.

'School? Bah!' scoffed Grumpa. 'I never went to school.'

'I like school,' said Ulrik. 'Shall I say you my seven times table?'

'What's the good of tables?' demanded Grumpa. 'Are they teaching you how to roar?'

'Dad gives me roaring lessons at home,' said Ulrik.

'Show Grumpa,' urged Mr Troll. 'Go on, Ulrik. Show him how you roar.'

Ulrik hesitated. He never did his best roars when he had an audience. Somehow it made him nervous and his throat dried up. However, his mum and dad were nodding at him eagerly and Grumpa was waiting. Ulrik clenched his fists and tromped up and down a few times, stamping his feet to gather himself. Taking a deep breath and pushing out his chest, he roared. 'Graaaaargh!'

His parents clapped. 'Lovely, Ulrik!' said Mrs Troll. 'Pretty scaresome, eh?' said Mr Troll.

Grumpa just scowled and folded his arms. 'Humph!' he said.

Later Ulrik lay in his parents' bed, trying to get to sleep. From across the landing he could hear the rumble of Grumpa's snores. Heavy footsteps came up the stairs. He closed his eyes, pretending to be asleep. The door creaked open.

'Look at him. Sleeping like a lambkins,' said Mrs Troll fondly.

'Too much like a lambkins if you ask me,' grumbled his dad's voice.

'Shhh!' said Mrs Troll. 'He'll hear you!'

Mr Troll peeled off his vest and threw it on the floor. He lowered his voice. 'Maybe Grumpa's right, it's our fault. Ulrik should be out tromping the forest with trolls of his own age.'

'He likes going to school. He's made friends,' said Mrs Troll. She sat down on the edge of the bed, which sagged to one side.

'I know,' said Mr Troll. 'But he just isn't . . . trollish.'

'His roar's improving,' said Mrs Troll.

'You heard him tonight. Feeble as a frog-hopper!' said Mr Troll, climbing into the bed. Ulrik heard the springs beneath him groan in protest.

'Stop worrying!' sighed Mrs Troll. 'Ulrik will be fine.' Mr Troll grunted and rolled over. Before long both of them were snoring.

Ulrik lay awake, squashed between his parents in the hollow of the mattress, thinking over what he'd just heard. He tried hard to be more trollish, but somehow he always seemed to get it wrong. It was true he couldn't roar like his dad and he didn't have a temper like his grumpa. If only he could do something to prove his trollishness to his parents. If only he could bags a goat and bring it home for supper!

Meet the Neighbours

THE NEXT MORNING Ulrik sat at the breakfast table, helping himself to Coco Pops out of the packet. He had set out all the bowls ready and made sure that none of them were clean. His mum was busy in the kitchen while his dad didn't seem to be up. Grumpa came downstairs, already dressed in his goatskin coat.

'Hello, Grumpa! Did you sleep well?' Ulrik asked. 'You were snoring.'

'Humph!' replied Grumpa. 'Where's your hat?'

'It's hanging up.'

'Run and fetch it then. We're going hunting. You and me.'

'Hunting? Uggsome!' said Ulrik.

When he returned his mum was spooning cold beans out of a can.

'Grumpa's taking me hunting, Mum!' said Ulrik.

'Hunting?' said Mrs Troll, alarmed. 'When was this decided?'

'I decided it just now,' said Grumpa.

'But where are you going to hunt?'

'In the forest,' replied Grumpa.

'Which forest, Grumpa?' asked Ulrik.

His mum gave him a meaningful look. '*You know*, Ulrik – the forest I was telling Grumpa about in my letters. The one where we always go.'

'Oh, *that* forest,' said Ulrik, nodding his head slowly. Now he understood. Grumpa thought there was a forest nearby where you could hunt goats, but actually there wasn't. He tried to hide his disappointment. For a moment he had believed he was going on his first hunting trip.

'Why don't you go tomorrow?' Mrs Troll suggested. 'I think it's going to rain.'

'Hogswoggle!' snorted Grumpa. 'A tiddly spot of

rain won't hurt us. I've been hunting when the snow's up to my bellies.'

'Yes, but you don't know the forest here,' said Mrs Troll. 'You might get lost.'

'I never get lost,' said Grumpa, buttoning his goatskin coat. 'Are you ready, Ulrik?'

Ulrik straightened his hunting hat. 'Ready.'

Mrs Troll stood in the doorway, blocking their

path. 'At least wait for Egbert. You don't even know the way.'

Luckily Mr Troll came downstairs at that moment and Mrs Troll explained – with a great deal of eye-rolling – that Grumpa wanted to take Ulrik hunting in the forest.

'The forest?' said Mr Troll, puzzled. 'Which forest?'

Ulrik could see they were going to have to go through the whole business all over again.

'You know, Dad, the one where we *always* go hunting.'

Mr Troll looked blank.

'The one I told Grumpa about in my letters, Eggy,' said Mrs Troll, attempting to wink and roll her eyes at the same time.

'Oh, *that* forest!' said Mr Troll, finally remembering. 'But they can't go there. Haven't you told him yet?'

It was Mrs Troll's turn to look blank. 'Told him what?'

'About the goblins!'

'Goblins?' said Grumpa. 'What are you blethering about?'

'Goblins as big as bears,' said Mr Troll.

'Yes! Terrible, scaresome goblins,' said Mrs Troll, catching on. 'They live underground.'

'They jump out and bite your toeses and won't let go.'

Grumpa stared at them both. 'I've never heard such a pile of cow-patties,' he said. 'Come on, Ulrik, we're going.' He opened the front door and strode down the path, with Ulrik trying to keep up. Mr and Mrs Troll exchanged worried looks and hurried after them.

At the gate Grumpa halted and looked left and right. 'Which way?' he demanded.

Mr Troll hesitated. 'Um . . . well, that depends . . .'

'Which way to the forest? It's a simple question!'

'Not really . . .'

Like most trolls Grumpa had very little patience – he had been scowling and grinding his fangs for some time, which was a sure sign that his temper was about to explode.

'Oh, for UGGNESS' SAKE!' he roared. 'I'll ask in here – maybe they talk some sense!'

With that he turned into the Priddles' driveway

and to the Trolls' horror marched up to the front door. Ulrik glanced back and saw his mum and dad, signalling to him frantically to do something. But what could he do? Grumpa was already hammering on the door with his fist.

Ulrik wondered how his mum and dad were going to explain this. The whole thing was getting very complicated. First Grumpa wanted to take him to an imaginary forest, now he wanted to meet the trolls next door who were actually peeples. Ulrik felt his mum should have thought of this when she was writing all those fibwoppers.

As luck would have it, no one answered the door.

'I think they're out, Grumpa,' said Ulrik.

Grumpa puzzled over the holly wreath on the front door which said 'Merry Christmas!'

'What's down there?' He pointed at the gravel path leading to the side gate.

'Oh, that goes to the back but we can't go in there, Grumpa . . .'

Too late. Grumpa had bulldozed through the gate and disappeared.

The back garden was empty and there was no sign of the Priddles when they peered through the French windows. Ulrik caught sight of a head peering at him over the garden fence. It was making some complicated hand signals, but he had no idea what they were supposed to mean.

'Maybe we should go, Grumpa,' he said anxiously.

'Hogswoggle!' replied Grumpa. 'They're trolls. They won't mind if we make ourselves at home.'

Grumpa rattled the back door. It was locked but that didn't stop him. He took a run at it and butted it with his head. There was a splintering of wood as the bolt buckled and the door gave way, falling inwards. They left it hanging by one hinge as they walked into the kitchen.

Grumpa stared at the rows of neat cupboards and the spotless cooker. He continued into the lounge, where he gaped at the cream-coloured carpet, the leather sofa and the TV in the corner.

'What kind of trolls are they?' he asked in disgust. 'It's clean! It smells sweet as buttercups!'

'Maybe they haven't dirtied it for a while,' said Ulrik. 'Come on, Grumpa – let's go!' He tugged at the sleeve of his coat. If the Priddles came back now and discovered them in the house, there would be all kinds of trouble.

Grumpa shook his head stubbornly. 'We'll go hunting later,' he said. 'First I want to meet these trolls. Someone needs to speak to them. They're living like peeples. It's disgustive!'

*

The Priddles' car turned into the drive and parked in front of the garage. Poking out of the boot was the Christmas tree they'd bought from the garden centre.

'Can we put it up now, Mum?' asked Warren excitedly.

'Of course we can, darling,' said Mrs Priddle. 'Help your dad to carry it through to the back.'

As they were dragging the tree out of the boot, Mr and Mrs Troll came rushing out of their house. They had seen the Priddles' car pull into the drive and were anxious to head them off.

'Piddle!' said Mr Troll.

'Can't stop – got to get this tree put up,' said Mr Priddle.

'Don't do it now,' said Mr Troll. 'Come round. Have some pots of tea.'

'No thanks!' said Mr Priddle, heading for the gate. 'We've had one.'

'Breakfast then!' said Mrs Troll. 'I've got eggs and jam.'

'Another time,' said Mrs Priddle. They disappeared through the side gate, leaving the Trolls looking after them helplessly.

Warren helped his dad carry the tree to the back door, where they halted unexpectedly. 'Ow!' cried Warren, getting tangled up with the rear end.

'Where's the back door?' asked Mr Priddle. He stared at the gap where the door used to be.

'Didn't you lock it when we went out?' asked Mrs Priddle.

'Of course I locked it! Look! Someone's broken it down!'

'Shhh!' Mrs Priddle held up a hand for silence. 'I can hear someone. They're inside!'

'Burglars!' gasped Warren.

Mrs Priddle clutched at her husband's arm. 'They're in the house! Call the police, Roger!'

Mr Priddle checked his pockets. 'I left my phone upstairs,' he groaned.

'What's it doing up there?'

'I don't know! I wasn't expecting to be burgled today!'

'See?' said Warren triumphantly. 'If I had a mobile phone, *I* could phone the police!'

'Be quiet, Warren!' hissed Mrs Priddle. 'What are we going to do? They're in there now stealing our things. My jewellery, Roger. The TV's brand new. And all the presents are on top of the wardrobe!'

'Are they?' said Warren, who had been trying to find them for some time.

'You'll just have to scare them off,' Mrs Priddle continued.

'Me?' said Mr Priddle. 'What if they're dangerous? They might be thugs! Criminals!'

'Of course they're criminals – they're burgling our house!' said Mrs Priddle. 'Make a lot of noise – that's what they say you should do.'

'Do they?' said Mr Priddle nervously. 'Don't they say you should wait for the police?'

'Roger! They're in our house! Are you just going to stand there and let them get away?'

Mr Priddle could see his wife was working herself into a temper. He wasn't sure if he would rather face her or the burglars. Screwing up his courage, he gripped the only weapon he had – the bushy green Christmas tree. It wasn't much but it would certainly give them a scratch or two.

'When I count to three, shout and make a racket,' he said.

'Can I shout "bogeys"?' asked Warren.

'Certainly not!' said Mrs Priddle.

'Shout anything! Just make it loud!' said Mr Priddle. He decided he was better holding the base of the Christmas tree – that way the burglars would get the pointy end. He took a deep breath. This was probably the bravest thing he'd ever done in his life – or the stupidest. 'I'm starting to count,' he said. 'One . . . two . . . three!'

'Arghhhh!' screamed Mrs Priddle.

'BOGEYS!' hollered Warren.

'Raaaaarrrrr!' roared Mr Priddle, charging in through the kitchen and shedding pine needles in all directions. He burst in through the lounge door and found he was running so fast that it was impossible to stop.

There was a loud BANG! followed by a shattering of glass as the point of the Christmas tree embedded itself in the screen of the new television.

Ulrik had leapt to his feet. So had Grumpa, who was roaring partly from fright and partly because trolls never miss a chance to roar.

Mr Priddle looked round slowly and saw a large elderly troll staring at him. He was dressed in a filthy coat and standing on their sofa.

'Who . . . who are you?' asked Mr Priddle.

'Never mind that,' growled Grumpa. 'Who the bogles are you?'

Ulrik looked from one face to the other. He could see this was going to take quite a bit of explaining.

Saving Trollmas

MR TROLL HAD BEEN trying to clamber over the back fence when he heard the bang from inside the house. He had hoped he could get Grumpa out before things got awkward, but the bang and the shouting told him he was too late.

When he and Mrs Troll finally went round to ring the doorbell it was answered by a very cross-looking Mrs Priddle. She had a good mind, she said, to report the whole matter to the police. If they couldn't control their elderly relatives, they ought to be kept indoors.

What did Grumpa think he was doing breaking into houses and stealing food from the fridge? (The remains of three chicken drumsticks had been found on the carpet.) The back door was hanging off and the new TV they'd bought for Christmas had shattered in a million pieces. (Mr Priddle pointed out he was partly to blame for the TV, but Mrs Priddle shouted at him not to interrupt.)

'And that isn't the worst of it,' she concluded. 'Do you know what he called me?'

'What?' sighed Mrs Troll.

'A pasty-faced peeples!' said Mrs Priddle. 'I've never been so insulted in my whole life.'

Mr Troll found this hard to believe – he could certainly think of some much better insults.

Once everyone had calmed down, the Trolls promised they would pay for the damage and returned to their own house. They sat at the breakfast table, trying to decide what to do. In all the confusion, Grumpa had disappeared.

'Where did he go?' asked Mrs Troll.

'I don't know! He just tromped off down the road,' replied Ulrik.

'Well, is he coming back?'

'He didn't say.' Ulrik propped his chin in his hands. It was partly his fault. He should have got Grumpa out of the house before the Priddles arrived. But it was difficult to persuade Grumpa to do anything – he was as stubborn as a mule and now he'd stormed off in a terrible sulk.

He looked at his mum. 'He will be all right, won't he?'

'Of course he will, my ugglesome. He's a grown troll. He's just in a bit of a temper, that's all.'

Mr Troll shook his head sadly. 'I don't blame him.'

'Oh, and who do *you* blame?' replied Mrs Troll irritably.

'Well, you,' said Mr Troll.

'ME?'

'Yes, you wrote him the letters!' said Mr Troll. 'You're the one telling all the fibwoppers!'

Mrs Troll snorted in disbelief. 'And have you ever stopped to think why?'

Mr Troll shrugged his shoulders. He had no idea.

'Because I wanted him to be proud of you!' said

Mrs Troll. 'I wanted him to think we live in a stinksome cave with nice trolls next door. I wanted him to imagine we have forests and mountains to look at and roast goat on the table every night.'

'But we don't!' said Mr Troll, puzzled.

'No, we don't,' replied Mrs Troll, her voice rising. 'We don't because we had to leave home. Because you, Egbert, got frighted by a billy goat on a bridge!'

'I was never frighted,' said Mr Troll indignantly.

'All right, beated, butted, whatever you want to call it.'

'GRARGH!' roared Mr Troll, standing up and kicking over his chair.

'Grargh yourself!' replied Mrs Troll.

Mr Troll stormed out of the room and slammed the door so hard that the clock fell off the wall.

Ulrik sighed. There was a long silence. It was always the same when his mum brought up the bridge thing. It ended with roaring and door-slamming.

His mum had gone to the window and was look-ing anxiously along the road. Ulrik tried to think of something to cheer her up. It was only five days until Trollmas. He was looking forward to that.

'Mum,' he said, 'can we have a tree?'

'What, my hairling?' said Mrs Troll absently.

'A tree. For Trollmas.'

'What do you want with a tree?'

'Peeples have trees in their houses. The Priddles have got one.'

'Really? What do you do with them?'

'You hang things on them,' explained Ulrik. 'Lights and shiny balls and socks.'

'Socks? You mean to dry them?'

'Maybe,' said Ulrik, who was a little hazy about the details. 'I think Warren said socks. You hang them on a tree and then you go to bed. And in the night, Father Trollmas comes and leaves you a sack.'

Mrs Troll looked bewildered. The strange habits of peeples never ceased to amaze her. 'But can we have one, Mum? A tree?' begged Ulrik.

'If you really want, my ugglesome. But just now we've got to find your grumpa.'

Ulrik nodded. 'Is he still staying for Trollmas?'

'Of course he is,' said Mrs Troll. She hoped he hadn't got into any trouble. He didn't know his way round and he had no experience of towns like Biddlesden. What if he wandered into the middle of the road or got arrested? Maybe Egbert ought to go and look for him.

'I know what would put Grumpa in a gladful mood,' said Ulrik.

'What?'

'A nice goat pie.'

Mrs Troll smiled. 'I wish I had one. It's nearly Trollmas and I still don't know where we're going to find a goat.'

Ulrik rested his chin on the table. 'It's a pity that farm can't give us one,' he said.

'What farm?'

'You know, the one I went to with school.'

Mrs Troll's eyes widened. She had forgotten all about Ulrik's trip to the farm last term. 'They had goats?' she said.

'I told you! There was one called Victor.'

'But lots of goats? A whole herd?'

'I think so.'

Mrs Troll clasped him by the cheeks and planted a wet kiss on his snout.

'You are my big, clever ugglesome!' she said. 'Wait till your dad hears this!'

'What are we going to do?' asked Ulrik.

'Do?' said Mrs Troll. 'You're going goat hunting – that's what you're going to do!'

Meanwhile Grumpa found himself lost in Biddlesden shopping arcade. He wasn't quite sure how he came to be there. After the shock of discovering there were peeples living next door, he had tromped off down the road in a temper, without the faintest idea where he was going. Somehow he had ended up on the high street and stumbled into the arcade.

Looking about him, he saw bright Christmas lights and crowds of shoppers bustling past. He wasn't used to peeples and he had never seen so many. They stared at him strangely and the smell of them made him sick and dizzy. He longed to see the handsome face of another troll.

Plunging on past shops, he didn't notice the sign saying 'Santa's Grotto', or hear the woman calling to him that he needed a ticket. Unexpectedly he found himself in the middle of a forest. It was made up of tall fir trees, all of them exactly the same and all glistening with snow. Magical music was playing somewhere. Maybe this was the forest his family had spoken about.

Following a path, he was startled to come on a group of rosy-cheeked, grinning goblins under a tree. They stood still as statues, their arms full of presents. Hoping to frighten them off, Grumpa growled. They didn't blink an eye. It was plain

they were under the spell of a witch or a wizard. Lost and anxious now, he hurried on, convinced he had stumbled into some enchanted forest by mistake. Round the bend he came upon a little log house, lit with fairy lights. Maybe whoever lived there could tell him the way out.

He passed through a silver bead curtain and came face to face with a fat peeples sitting in a chair. He was wearing a bright red suit and cap. A flowing white beard hung over his round belly.

'Ho ho!' boomed Father Christmas. 'And what

do you . . . ?' He broke off. Instead of the eager children he was expecting, an ugly, wild-eyed troll stood before him. Its lips parted, revealing sharp fangs. Father Christmas raised his hands to show he meant no harm.

Grumpa stepped back – the fat wizard was about to cast a spell! He backed away, stumbling over a mound of presents. 'Please! I won't tell anybodies,' he mumbled.

In a second he was back through the bead curtain and running through the forest. If he ever made it back to Mountain View, he vowed he would shut the door and stay in his room. Biddlesden was a far more dangerous place than he could have imagined.

Night Raiders

LATER THAT NIGHT Ulrik and Mr Troll stole across a field under the cover of darkness. Ulrik had already trodden in a cow-pattie because it was hard to see where you were going in the dark. He felt very nervous and excited. It was long past his bedtime, but here he was on a dangerous hunting trip with his dad. His only worry was that they might meet one of the farm peeples. A single light shone from a top window of Longbottom Farm.

Ulrik pulled down the goatskin hat his grumpa

had given him. Grumpa would be asleep now, back at the house.

To tell the truth, Ulrik was a bit worried about him. Earlier that evening he had turned up, looking pale and exhausted. He had babbled something about a hairy-faced wizard who had tried to put a spell on him. Ulrik thought he must have been watching TV. Still, a nice goat pie would cheer him up. Ulrik sniffed the air – the goats were not far away.

They stole along the side of a long, rust-coloured barn. Mr Troll put a finger to his lips and

they listened for a moment. From inside the barn came animal sounds of shuffling and grunting.

'Goatses,' said Mr Troll, baring his fangs in a smile. 'You wait here, Ulrik.'

'But Dad –'

'Just do as I say . . .' Mr Troll was already creeping forward to the corner of the barn. A moment later he was swallowed by the dark.

Ulrik waited, listening. He heard the sound of his dad running, then a deafening crash as he hit something. Then a roar and a loud angry squealing. A moment later his dad appeared again, panting for breath and with mud and straw in his hair.

'Pigses!' he gasped. 'Great big snorkers!'

'That's what I was trying to tell you, Dad,' said Ulrik. 'The goats aren't in this barn, they're over there!'

They found the goats in the yard behind the farmhouse, penned in by a stone wall. Ulrik counted fourteen in all, including one skinny brown kid lying next to its mother.

'Don't be frighted,' said Mr Troll, as they crouched by the wall.

'I'm not,' replied Ulrik.

'Good,' said Mr Troll. 'Because goats can always smell a frighted troll. That's when they charge and butt you with their hornses.'

Ulrik guessed his dad was thinking about the last time he'd tackled a goat – the giant billy goat which had tossed him off the bridge into the dark, swirling river. These goats didn't look too big, although they did have horns between their ears.

'This is a chance for you to practise roaring, Ulrik,' said Mr Troll. 'You slip inside the gate and give them a great, scaresome roar. Send them running to me and I'll be waiting to catch a fat one in the sack.'

'What if I fright them?' asked Ulrik.

'You're meant to fright them!'

'Couldn't I sing to them instead?'

Mr Troll rolled his eyes. 'We've been over this, Ulrik.'

'Or I could feed them some biscuits.'

Mr Troll gave him a look. 'Are we hunting goatses or making friends with them?'

'Hunting, Dad.'

'Then let's get on with it.'

Ulrik crawled on all fours to the end of the wall

and slunk over to the gate. It opened with a creak and he slipped inside. The goats took no notice of him. He could see his dad's shadow at the far end of the pen, waiting with the sack at the ready. All he had to do was make them run from him. Easy-cheesy. He clenched his fists and screwed his eyes tight shut. 'Grarrgh!' he roared.

It wasn't his best roar – he was worried the peeples in the farmhouse might hear – and it didn't have much effect. The nearest goat raised its head and blinked at him, then they all went back to chewing the grass or continued to sleep. His dad signalled to him to try again. He took a deep breath. This time he stamped his feet at the same time as he roared. It made no difference – the goats only turned their backs and went on eating.

Mr Troll came running back. 'What the bogles are you doing?' he hissed.

'Roaring softlys. I didn't want to wake the peeples.'

'You won't even wake the goats like that!' said Mr Troll. 'Here – hold the sack. Let me do the roaring.'

His dad flitted off into the dark again, leaving Ulrik holding the empty sack.

He was just wondering whether to close the gate when a fearsome noise broke the stillness.

'GRAAAAARGHHHH!'

The roar of a hunting troll is a sound to chill the blood. It's enough to make a giant dive under the covers clutching his teddy bear. To the sleepy,

unsuspecting goats it sounded like a tiger on the loose. They pricked up their ears, turned tail and stampeded towards the gate.

Ulrik saw them thundering towards him: a blur of hooves and horns and dust. He held the sack at the ready but it was hopeless. There were fourteen goats and only one of him – he might as well have tried to catch a swarm of bees in a paper bag.

The goats were running for their lives and they had seen the open gate. This was their chance of freedom.

In the farmhouse, Mr and Mrs Douglas sat bolt upright in bed. The animals in the yard were making a terrible din – bleating, braying and clucking as if the world was coming to an end.

'It's that damn fox! The varmint!' said Mr Douglas, jumping out of bed. He struggled with his trousers, hopping around the room trying to get both feet into one leg. 'This time I'll have him! I'll blast him!'

Mrs Douglas pulled back the curtains. 'The goats have got out!' she cried. 'They're in the yard!'

'What?' said Mr Douglas. 'He's after the goats? The cheeky beggar! I'll pepper his backside!' He finally got his trousers on and thumped down the stairs to find his boots. By the back door he reached into the cupboard for his rifle.

In the yard, Ulrik was out of breath. Goats were a lot harder to catch than he'd expected. They bucked and kicked when you caught them by the tail. They left a trail of goat droppings which made the yard as slippery as an ice rink. With all the dashing and crashing around they seemed to have woken every animal in the farm. Dogs barked, pigs squealed and a horse kicked at its stable door.

Ulrik wondered where his dad was. In the confusion he had dropped the sack and now he couldn't find it.

A head poked out from the corner of a water trough and two bright eyes blinked at him. It was the skinny brown kid he'd noticed before. Ulrik reached into his pocket and brought out a biscuit. 'Here, little ninny goat,' he said softly, holding out some crumbs. The kid took half a step towards him. Ulrik squatted down to its level to make himself seem smaller. He began to hum softly. Amazingly, the goat trotted closer and licked the crumbs from his hand. 'Good girl!' said Ulrik.

'DON'T MOVE!' commanded a voice behind him. He looked round to see the farmer, dressed in a pyjama top and baggy trousers, aiming the barrel of a rifle at him. Ulrik had never seen a rifle before but he knew they weren't for tickling.

Mr Douglas, for his part, had never seen a troll before and finding one in his yard in the middle of the night scared the life out of him. He was prepared for foxes, but he had never seen anything like this ugly brute with the savage fangs.

The rifle shook in his hands. The hairy creature took a step towards him. 'Back! Get back!' warned Mr Douglas. But his next words were lost as everything was plunged into darkness. Someone had jammed a foul-smelling sack over his head.

'Run!' bellowed Mr Troll, who had crept up behind the farmer.

Ulrik ran across the yard with his heart pounding and his dad close behind him. When they had crossed three fields, plunged through a ditch and climbed a wall, they came out on a country lane. Mr Troll bent over, hands on knees, trying to catch his breath.

'Uggsome! Is hunting always like that?' panted Ulrik.

Mr Troll shook his head, too breathless to speak.

'Did I do OK?' asked Ulrik. 'I nearly caught a kiddler but the farmer frighted it off.'

'Maybe we . . . need more . . . roaring practice,' panted Mr Troll. He broke off and listened. Footsteps were coming down the lane. What now? Maybe they hadn't given the farmer the slip after all.

Mr Troll looked around wildly for a place to hide and settled for pulling Ulrik down in the long grass by the side of the road.

'Are we stopping for a rest?' whispered Ulrik.

'Shh! Someone's coming!'

The footsteps drew closer, a light *trip trop* on the

road. They stopped. Mr Troll imagined the farmer with his rifle in his hand, sniffing the air to catch their scent. In future he'd remember to wear a clean vest for hunting.

Once again the footsteps came, nearer and nearer. A shadow appeared above them and two bright eyes blinked in the dark.

'She followed us!' said Ulrik, delighted.

'Well I'll be bogled!' said Mr Troll. 'It's a goat!'

Hiding Rosemary

MRS PRIDDLE WOKE from a lovely
dream. She was throwing a Christmas
party at her house and all kinds of famous people
were there. She was just about to tell the Queen
a funny joke when something woke her up. It was
the kind of noise Warren made when he ate with
his mouth open – *chomp, chomp, chomp*. She
turned to glare at her husband, who was lying on
his side with his mouth lolling open.

'Roger!' she said.

'Mmm?' said her husband, still half asleep.

'Stop making that noise!'

'I wasn't!' mumbled Mr Priddle.

'You were chewing in my ear!'

Mr Priddle rolled over, presenting his back to her. 'Go back to shleep,' he grunted.

Chomp, chomp, chomp! Mrs Priddle heard it again. She hadn't dreamed it – she was wide awake now. The chomping, chewing noise wasn't in the bedroom at all, it was coming from outside the window. 'It's those trolls again!' she said out loud.

Ever since they'd moved in next door the Trolls were always disturbing her sleep. They thumped and clumped around as if they were dragging bodies up and down stairs (something Mrs Priddle thought was quite likely). They roared in the back garden at seven o' clock in the morning and waved cheerily at her husband when he shouted at them to stop. Now, by the sound of it, they were having a picnic on her front lawn.

Mrs Priddle climbed out of bed and pulled back the curtains.

'There's a goat!' she said in astonishment.

'Tell him I'm asleep,' mumbled Mr Priddle.

'Roger, there's a goat in our garden eating my winter jasmine!'

Mr Priddle groaned. 'You're dreaming,' he mumbled. But his wife yanked the duvet off him and shook him until he opened his eyes. 'Come and see for yourself!'

Mr Priddle staggered to the window, rubbing the sleep from his eyes. Looking out, he saw a skinny brown goat contentedly munching its way through their shrubbery. At one time, he thought, this was a perfectly normal neighbourhood. You could look out of your window in the morning and see the paper boy passing on his bike. Now it was trolls or goats in your garden.

'Don't just stand there!' said his wife at his shoulder. 'Go down and shoo him away!'

'Why me?' asked Mr Priddle. 'Why don't you do the shooing for a change?'

'I'm not dressed for it!' said Mrs Priddle. 'I'm in my nightie!'

Warren poked his head round the bedroom door. 'Dad! Guess what?' he said excitedly. 'There's a goat in our garden!'

Mr Priddle opened the front door and padded nervously into the garden, wearing his dressing gown and slippers. Warren was watching him with interest from the kitchen window.

'Hey!' said Mr Priddle. The goat's head appeared above one of the bushes. It had horns – small ones, but horns nevertheless. 'Shoo!' said Mr Priddle, keeping his distance. 'Shoo!'

He clapped his hands. The goat seemed to think this was an invitation to get to know each other better. It came trotting eagerly towards him.

'No! I said shoo! GO AWAY!' said Mr Priddle, backing towards the door. The belt of his dressing gown was dangling loose and suddenly the goat

dipped its head and made a grab for it. It seized
the belt in its mouth and began to pull.

'Let go, you brute!' said Mr Priddle. It was either
an undignified tug of war with a goat or abandon
his dressing gown altogether. He hoped that none
of the neighbours were watching.

'Piddle!' boomed a familiar voice. 'You found her!'

Two large hairy heads appeared above the front hedge. Mr Priddle groaned – he might have known the trolls were responsible for this.

'Rosemary!' scolded Ulrik. 'Naughty goats! I told you to stay in the garden.'

'She's been eating my plants!' grumbled Mr Priddle. 'Not to mention my dressing gown.'

'Goatses eat anything,' nodded Mr Troll. 'Grasses, berries, even dressing-gongs.'

'I don't care what they eat. I want to know what's she doing in my garden!' said Mr Priddle.

'She got out,' explained Mr Troll. 'We tied her to the fence but she bited through the rope.'

'But what's she doing here? Where on earth did you get a goat?'

Ulrik was about to explain about the farm, but Mr Troll hastily cut him off. 'Oh, the post peeples brought her,' he said.

'The postman?' said Mr Priddle. 'The postman brought you a goat?'

'Yes. She's a present,' said Mr Troll. Rosemary had spotted the holly wreath on the Priddles' door and was now standing on her hind legs, trying to reach it.

'Leave that alone!' said Mr Priddle sharply. 'You can't keep a goat round here. You need a licence.'

'Oh, we're not going to keep her,' said Mr Troll.

'Aren't we?' said Ulrik.

'No, no – goats is for eating. A young kid is tastesome, especially in a pie. We always have goat pie on Trollmas Day.'

Ulrik put his hands over Rosemary's ears. He thought his dad might at least keep his voice down. 'Come on, Rosemary – let's find you some breakfast,' he said.

Mr Priddle watched them go, re-tying the soggy belt of his dressing gown. 'And in future kindly keep her out of my garden!' he called after them.

Back home the Trolls discussed what to do while Rosemary trotted through the downstairs rooms in search of something else to eat. For a young kid she certainly seemed to have a healthy appetite.

'Why can't she stay in the garden?' asked Ulrik. 'She likes it there.'

'That's no good,' said Mr Troll. 'She'll only run

off again. And anyway, Grumpa is bound to see her. We don't want to spoil the surprise.' They had decided not to tell Grumpa about Rosemary yet. Mr Troll was looking forward to seeing his delighted face on Trollmas Day when he found that goat pie was on the menu.

Mrs Troll glanced over at Rosemary as she licked some dried bean juice off the wall.

'I suppose we could just . . . you know . . .' she said.

'What?' said Mr Troll.

Mrs Troll lowered her voice. 'Cook her now.'

'NO!' protested Ulrik.

'She's only a goat, hairling,' said Mrs Troll. 'She's got to be eaten!'

'Can't we just keep her until Trollmas?' pleaded Ulrik.

'But where, my ugglesome?' said Mrs Troll. 'Where can we hide a goat?'

'I know! The bathroom,' said Ulrik. 'Grumpa never goes in there.'

'That's true,' said Mr Troll. 'He'd rather kiss a goblin than have a wash.'

'Someone would have to feed her,' said Mrs Troll doubtfully.

'I'll do it, Mum!' said Ulrik eagerly. 'I'll go in every day.'

Mrs Troll considered. 'Well, she could do with a bit of fattening up,' she said. 'We don't want stringy goat in our pie!'

After supper that evening Ulrik slipped upstairs to the bathroom while no one was paying any attention. Under his jumper he had concealed a bowl of food. His parents and Grumpa were downstairs arguing in the kitchen.

Since his trip into town, Grumpa seemed more

ill-tempered than ever. He complained that the cave they lived in was too large and the rooms were too dry and stinkless. The streets were full of pasty-faced peeples and he kept asking when he was going to meet another troll. Most of the time he sulked in his room, appearing only for meals. Ulrik could tell Grumpa was getting on his parents' nerves, but at least it would be Trollmas soon and everyone would be happy.

He opened the bathroom door. Rosemary got to her feet, pleased to see him. Little bits of the shower curtain littered the floor. He brought out the food he'd carefully prepared. His dad had said goats ate everything, so he'd brought a bit of anything he could find. There was some cold baked bean, a carrot, some broken biscuits and a small mound of Coco Pops. As an afterthought, he'd sprinkled a handful of grass on top.

'There we are, little kiddler,' he said, placing the bowl in the bath.

Rosemary sniffed the food and began to eat hungrily. In a couple of minutes the bowl had been licked clean and she was nosing into Ulrik's pockets.

'Sorry, that's all I've got,' said Ulrik, patting her head. 'Time for bed now.'

Rosemary's brown eyes blinked back at him. 'Bed!' said Ulrik. 'Sleepy-bogles.'

He climbed into the bath and lay down, closing his eyes to show what he meant. Rosemary bent over and licked his face with her rough warm tongue.

'No, no!' giggled Ulrik. 'You in bath – go sleepy-leepy.'

He picked Rosemary up and set her down, struggling, in the bath. The goat blinked at him puzzled. Ulrik had an idea. When he was small and he couldn't get to sleep his mum used to sing him an old trollaby*. He began to croon it softly now.

*'Sleep troggler grunting,
Daddy's gone a-hunting.
Gone to bags a goats's skin,
To wrap the tiny troggler in.'*

Maybe he should have picked a song with better

---

* *Trollaby – bedtime song.*

words but the trollaby seemed to do the trick. Rosemary folded her legs under her and lay down in the bath to listen. Her brown eyes began to droop and her head nodded forward. Ulrik went on singing until she was asleep. The door opened and his dad looked in.

'What are you doing?'

'Shhh! Singing Rosemary to sleep,' whispered Ulrik.

Mr Troll closed the door behind him and looked at the goat dozing in the bath. 'I wish you'd stop calling her Rosemary,' he said.

'Why?' asked Ulrik.

'Because she's a goat! Goatses don't have names.'

'Why don't they?' persisted Ulrik.

'Because they're for eating, Ulrik. You can't cook someone called Rosemary!'

'Shhh! She'll hear you!'

He sat down on the side of the bath. Mr Troll could tell that something was bothering him.

'Dad, how do you . . . you know . . . before you put them in the pie?'

'Swizzle them?' said Mr Troll. 'Well, some trolls use their bare hands but, myselves, I've always used a rock. A rock does a nice quick jobs. One bash on the head and –'

'Dad!' Ulrik had covered his ears.

'What?' said Mr Troll. 'You've got to learn some-time. I was thinking you could help me.'

'No!' Ulrik shook his head sullenly. 'Anyway, why do we have to eat goat?'

'Why?' Mr Troll couldn't believe his ears.

'Because we're trolls! Trolls eat goatses.'

'But there are lots of other things we could eat,' Ulrik argued.

'Nothing as tastesome as goat pie. It's always been your favourite, ever since you were a little troggler.'

Ulrik shrugged. 'I think I've changed my mind. From now on I'm going to be a veggy-tellyum.'

'A veggy . . . what the bogles is that?' asked Mr Troll.

'Alice Snorley, in my class, is one. It's when you don't eat meat.'

'DON'T EAT MEAT??' This was too much for Mr Troll. He stormed out of the bathroom, clumped downstairs and burst out of the back door. His roar could be heard halfway down the road.

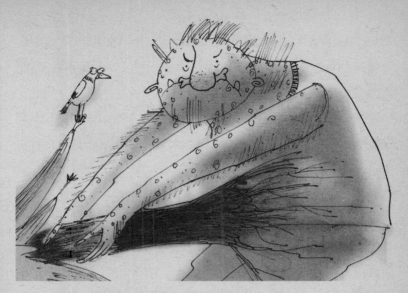

Goat on the Loose

MR TROLL PLODDED along the road with his head down, dragging the giant tree by its roots. People coming the other way had to leap off the pavement in order to avoid being swept into the gutter, but Mr Troll hardly noticed because he was thinking about Ulrik.

Grumpa was right, he said to himself. It was his fault that Ulrik wasn't more trollish. It was hardly surprising. Instead of playing in a forest like any normal troll he had to go to a school and sit in a classroom saying his seven times tables all day. It was bound to get him muddled. Now he was calling goats Rosemary and talking about turning into a veggy-smelly-thing.

It was terrible! Shameful! He never thought he'd see the day when a son of his refused to eat goat. If Grumpa ever found out he would go raving blunkers. 'WON'T EAT GOAT?' he'd roar. 'Is he a troll or a rabbit?' Grumpa had eaten his first goat as soon as he'd got his baby fangs. In any case, Mr Troll had given it a lot of thought and he'd decided that the truth was Ulrik was missing home. Homesickness did funny things to you – it got you muddled and your eyes started leaking.

That's why he'd hit on the idea of the tree. Ulrik had been begging them for a tree and Mr Troll had found the perfect one. It was a giant Norway Spruce, green and bushy and smelling like the forest at the foot of Troll Mountain. It had taken him two hours to dig it up. There had been a bit of a tug of war with the park keeper, which Mr Troll had enjoyed, though he won too easily.

He dragged the tree down the drive and came to a halt. The only thing he hadn't worked out was how to get it through the front door.

'Arggh! Gnhhhhh!' he grunted, heaving with all his strength.

'What the bogles are you doing?' asked Mrs Troll, coming into the hall.

'I brought a tree,' said Mr Troll, wiping the sweat from his brow.

'I can see that. Why are you bashing the door down with it?'

'Ulrik wanted a tree for Trollmas. You stand them in the window.'

Mrs Troll climbed over the dirty roots of the fir tree and inspected the green bushy part. One end was jammed in the doorway while the other was still out on the street.

'Eggy! It's huge!' she said.

'I know!' grinned Mr Troll. 'I didn't want a tiddler.'

'Well, you'll never get it in here – you'll have to put it in the back garden!'

Ulrik was feeding Rosemary in the bathroom when he saw the shadow of a giant tree swaying outside the window. He left Rosemary's bowl on the floor, dashed downstairs and out into the garden.

'Wow! It's uggnormous!' he exclaimed.

Mr Troll was packing earth around the tree's roots. It was leaning drunkenly to one side but he thought this could be sorted out later.

'You wanted a tree,' he said. 'This is like the ones we grow back home, Ulrik.'

'Can I hang things on it?'

Mr Troll waved a hand airily. 'You can do what you like. It's yours.'

Ulrik set to work. He didn't have any fairy lights or coloured balls, so he decorated his Trollmas tree with whatever he could find. He hung his socks on the branches, adding a vest and a pair of his mum's extra-large knickers for good measure. Christmas trees were meant to be bright and colourful and this one certainly was. He was so absorbed in what he was doing that he didn't notice Warren Priddle staring at him over the fence.

'What is *that*?' pointed Warren.

'Oh, hello, Warren. Dad got me a tree!' said Ulrik proudly.

Warren gazed up at the gigantic fir tree which rose almost as high as the house.

'It hasn't got any lights,' he pointed out. 'Or a fairy on the top.'

'No, but I used all my socks,' said Ulrik. 'I hung them up like you said.'

'It's stockings not socks,' said Warren scornfully. 'And you're meant to hang them on your bed. Don't you know anything about Christmas?'

'Not really,' admitted Ulrik cheerfully. 'I think Trollmas is different.'

Warren was looking round the garden. 'What have you done with that goat?' he asked.

'Rosemary?'

'Yes. My dad says you've eaten her.'

'No, she's in the bathroom,' said Ulrik. 'It's a secret. We don't want my grumpa . . .' He broke off. A startled cry had come from the house.

'What was that?' asked Warren. Ulrik looked up at his bedroom window. A worrying thought crossed his mind. Five minutes ago he had been feeding Rosemary in the bathroom, but he'd been distracted by the sight of the tree at the window. In his excitement, had he remembered to close the door behind him? Surely he had.

Grumpa's face appeared at his bedroom window.

'Help! There's a wild goat in here!'

Maybe he hadn't.

'Hadn't you better go and help him?' asked
Warren, gazing up at the window.

'He'll be all right,' replied Ulrik. 'Grumpa's used
to catching goats. He isn't frighted of anything.'

'Oh no?' said Warren. 'He looks pretty scared to
me.'

It was true that the fearless goat-hunter was

behaving quite oddly. Grumpa was standing on the windowsill and had pulled the curtains round him for protection. Ulrik could hear Rosemary's excited bleating – she probably thought he had biscuits in his pockets. He caught a glimpse of her head at the window.

'Wait there, Grumpa!' he called.

But Grumpa had decided that 'waiting there' with a savage goat trying to bite his feet was out of the question. He opened the window and gingerly stepped out on to the ledge, edging towards the drainpipe.

'Look out!' said Warren. 'He's going to jump!'

They both watched spellbound as Grumpa inched his way along the ledge. Halfway along his foot slipped and he was left clinging to the drainpipe with his feet dangling in mid-air. Rosemary poked her head out of the window and bleated.

'Get away!' cried Grumpa, kicking out in alarm. Ulrik doubted this was a good idea. Most drainpipes are not built to take the weight of a fully grown troll and this one was no exception. With a cracking, groaning sound the pipe started to come away from the wall.

'Watch out, Grumpa!' warned Ulrik.

Grumpa had felt the drainpipe moving and caught hold of the only thing that was to hand – which happened to be a giant Norway Spruce. For a few seconds he clung to the top, like a life-size Christmas fairy. Then, as if in slow motion, the tree began to topple sideways.

'ARGGHHHH!' cried Grumpa.

It was lucky there was something to break his fall on the other side of the fence. It was not so lucky that the something was the Priddles' new greenhouse. There was a mighty crash – followed

by several smaller crashes as the remainder of the roof fell in and the sides collapsed like a folding deckchair.

Ulrik and Warren ran over to the fence to see what had happened.

'Blunking bogles!' said Ulrik.

The tree had flattened a section of the Priddles' fence but that was the least of the damage. Grumpa was sitting in the remains of a greenhouse, surrounded by socks, shattered glass and broken flower-pots. Part of the Christmas tree had snapped off and he was still clinging to it uselessly. On his head sat Mrs Troll's extra-large knickers.

Ulrik of course got the blame. His mum and dad blamed him for leaving the bathroom door open. Grumpa complained he should have been warned there was a goat on the loose. The Priddles came out into the garden to join in with all the pointing, roaring and shouting. In the middle of it all Mrs Priddle picked up a broken flower-pot and burst into tears. 'It's meant to be Christmas!' she sobbed. 'Christmas!'

This put an end to the shouting and everyone looked at their feet awkwardly. Mr Priddle took his wife inside to make her a strong cup of tea while the Trolls returned to their house, feeling sorry about Mrs Priddle and her ruined Christmas.

In all the commotion they had forgotten about Rosemary. They found her in the kitchen, hoovering up spilled Coco Pops from the floor.

'This can't go on,' said Mrs Troll, sitting down heavily. 'She's driving me up the road.'

'Me too!' agreed Mr Troll. 'And we'll have to pay for the Piddles' greenshouse.'

'That wasn't her fault!' Ulrik pointed out.

Grumpa limped in and sat down. 'Don't bother about me,' he said bitterly. 'I could have broken my neck but don't worry about that!'

'She didn't mean any harm, Grumpa,' said Ulrik. 'You must have frighted her!'

'Humph!' said Grumpa.

'Ulrik,' said Mr Troll, 'take Rosemary outside!'

'But Dad –' protested Ulrik.

'Outside!' ordered Mr Troll.

Ulrik did as he was told. He sat on the fallen fir tree, trying to listen to what his parents were saying in the kitchen. He caught the words 'pie' and 'blunking goat' several times.

Rosemary seemed to know something was wrong and tried to cheer him up by licking his ear. He stroked her head. 'It's not your fault, is it?' he said. 'You were just hungry.'

The goat regarded him with trusting brown eyes.

Tomorrow was Trollmas Eve, when his mum would start baking the pie for the big day. Rosemary's time was running out. Ulrik glanced back at the house and made up his mind.

Ten minutes later, Mr Troll came outside to look for him.

'Ulrik!' he said. 'Ulrik, where are you?' He looked around.

The back gate was open.

On the Run

ON BIDDLESDEN High Street people were doing their last-minute Christmas shopping. Everyone seemed to be in a hurry and pushed past, carrying bags and looking tired and impatient.

Ulrik kept bumping into people. Although he had Rosemary on a lead she seemed to be leading him rather than the other way round. He stopped outside the window of a bakery to gaze hungrily at the mince pies and jolly snowmen biscuits. In his pocket he had one sticky chocolate biscuit left but he was saving that for supper.

Rosemary pressed her nose up against the window and tried to lick an iced bun through the glass.

'Sorry, I can't buy you anything,' said Ulrik. 'I haven't got any peas*.'

The pair of them seemed to be attracting some strange looks from passers-by. Ulrik wondered if it was obvious he was running away from home.

Past the shopping centre, they came to a set of steps leading down into a dark passageway. Ulrik had slept in the subway once with his mum and dad. His dad said its sweet, stinksome smell reminded him of their cave back home. Ulrik led Rosemary down. He could hear the rumble of cars passing overhead and the *trip trop* of people's feet as they hurried by.

Rosemary bleated and nuzzled in his pockets, searching for something else to eat.

'All right, you greedy goat,' said Ulrik.

He broke the chocolate biscuit in two. One half

---

* *Peas – money (as in 10 peas)*

he ate hungrily while he let Rosemary lick the remaining crumbs from his other hand. In a few seconds it was all gone. Ulrik wondered when it would start getting dark. It seemed like hours since they'd left home.

'What are we going to do now?' he asked. 'I can't take you back or you'll end up in a pie. Maybe we should try and get you home. Would you like that? You could play with all the other goatses.' Rosemary blinked at him and licked his face to see if any crumbs were stuck to it.

Ulrik heard the echo of feet descending the steps. He shrank back in the shadows, putting an arm round Rosemary to calm her. Suddenly the subway didn't seem such a safe place to hide. The footsteps drew nearer and halted.

'Hello – who's this? Aren't you Ulrik?'

Ulrik nodded. He had seen the policewoman before, the time she had brought his dad home in a panda car.

'What are you doing here?' she asked.

'I've run away from home,' said Ulrik.

'Is that right? And what about your four-legged friend – has she run away too?'

Ulrik nodded. 'This is Rosemary. My mum and dad want to cook her in a pie.'

'Oh, I'm sure they don't!' said the policewoman.

'They do,' said Ulrik. 'Goat pie is tastesome – at least I used to think so but now I'm a veggytellyum.'

'I see,' said the policewoman. 'So you thought you'd better run away. Where were you planning to sleep tonight?'

'I don't know yet,' admitted Ulrik. 'This isn't so bad.'

The policewoman sniffed. 'A bit damp and smelly,' she said. 'Tell you what, have you had anything to eat?'

'Only three biscuits,' admitted Ulrik. 'That's all I could bring.'

'Why don't you come down the station with me?' asked the policewoman. 'I'm sure we can rustle up some lemonade and a bit of cake.'

Ulrik considered. 'What kind of cake?'

'What kind do you like?'

'Chocolate,' said Ulrik. 'Rosemary likes that too.'

'Chocolate it is, then,' said the policewoman. 'I'll just radio the sarge and tell him we're on our way.'

An hour later Ulrik was sipping lemonade in a room at the police station. There was a knock at the door. It was Sergeant Blott, who had been looking after them.

'Someone to see you,' he said.

Mr and Mrs Troll burst in, looking greatly relieved.

'Ulrik! Are you all right, my ugglesome?' asked Mrs Troll, hugging him tightly.

'He's fine,' said Sergeant Blott. 'I've never seen chocolate cake disappear so fast.'

Mrs Troll seized the sergeant in a hug. 'Thank

you for finding him!' she said, planting a kiss on his bald head. The sergeant turned a deep shade of pink and struggled to escape. He found himself face to face with Mr Troll, who opened his arms.

'No! No more kissing!' said the sergeant hastily. 'Just take him home and try to keep him out of subways in future.'

'We will,' promised Mrs Troll. She put an arm round Ulrik and gave him a squeeze.

'Come on, hairling – you must be starving.'

But Ulrik hung back. 'What about Rosemary?' he asked.

Everyone looked at Rosemary, who had finished off the cake crumbs on the plate and was now nibbling the corner of a poster on the wall. Ulrik called her and she trotted over at the sound of her name. Seeing Mr Troll, she sniffed his hand and began to lick it.

'Ha ha! Stop it – that tickles!' laughed Mr Troll.

'See, Dad – she's pleased to see you,' said Ulrik. He stroked Rosemary's head.

'You promise you're not going to eat her?'

Mr and Mrs Troll exchanged looks.

'We can't, Eggy,' said Mrs Troll. 'Not now.'

'Can't we?' said Mr Troll.

'Look at them!' They both looked. Ulrik had his arms round Rosemary's neck and the goat was nuzzling up to him. She gazed at them with her innocent brown eyes.

Sergeant Blott sniffed and pulled a hanky from his pocket.

'You mean no goat pie?' said Mr Troll.

Mrs Troll shook her head.

'Not even on Trollmas Day?'

'We'll just have to go without this year.'

Mr Troll sighed. 'Back to blunking bean again.'

'Does that mean you promise?' asked Ulrik.

'We promise,' nodded Mrs Troll. 'Maybe we should take Rosemary back to the farm where she belongs.'

Ulrik ran to his parents and hugged them each in turn. 'Thanks, Dad! Thanks, Mum!' Sergeant Blott dabbed his eyes and pretended he needed to blow his nose.

'There's just one thing,' said Mr Troll as they left the police station. 'How are we going to explain this to Grumpa?'

Hairy Weakling

'**N**OT EAT HER?' said Grumpa when he heard the news.

'No,' said Mr Troll rather sheepishly. 'We've decided to take her back.'

'You've lost your bogles!' said Grumpa. 'You're mad as a sack of goblins. She's a goat!'

'I know, Dad, but –'

'Trolls eat goats,' Grumpa went on, tromping up and down and waving his arms. 'We hunt them and catch them and cook them in pies. That's what trolls do!'

'I know . . .' said Mr Troll.

'And what about tomorrow? You promised me a pie! You can't have Trollmas Day without goat pie!'

'We'll open a nice can of bean,' said Mrs Troll. 'Maybe with some fish's fingers.'

Grumpa gaped at her. 'Fingers? Bean? On Trollmas Day?'

'I'm sorry,' said Mrs Troll. 'I know it's not the same, but Ulrik's so fond of Rosemary. It just wouldn't be right to eat her.'

Grumpa slumped down into an armchair. The shock was too much to take in. His own family! His own grandson – friends with a goat! What would his friends at home say if they ever got to hear of it?

'Well,' he said, regarding Mr Troll darkly, 'I suppose it's only to be expected. He's just like his dad – harmless as a hedgepig.'

'Me?' growled Mr Troll. 'Are you calling me harmless?'

Mrs Troll sighed. Sooner or later she knew it would end in an argument.

'Harmless! Meekling! Hairy weakling!' said Grumpa, warming to his theme.

Mr Troll glared at his dad and the two faced each other snout to snout.

'Eggy's not a weakling,' objected Mrs Troll.

'Oh no?' said Grumpa. 'Isn't that why you had to move? Because he runs away from ninny goats?'

Mr Troll bristled. 'I didn't run away,' he said. 'I was butted off a bridge.'

'And look where it's got you,' said Grumpa. 'Living next door to peeples! It's shamesome. Since I got here I haven't met one single troll. Not one! So tell me – where are they all hiding?'

Mr Troll sighed deeply. It was no use trying to pretend any longer. 'There aren't any,' he said.

'Ha! I thought so. And all this blether about hunting in forests!'

'I made it up,' admitted Mrs Troll. 'We found Rosemary on a peeples' farm.'

'You see?' Grumpa jabbed a stubby finger. 'Nothing but a pack of fibwoppers! Call yourself trollish? I'm ashamed of you. You're too frighted even to come home.'

Ulrik had been listening while he fed a carrot to

Rosemary. Now he looked up. 'Anyway,' he said, 'all trolls get frighted sometimes.'

'Hogswoggle!' snorted Grumpa. 'I've never been frighted in my life!'

'Yes you have, Grumpa,' Ulrik reminded him. 'Remember this morning when Rosemary got into your room?'

Grumpa suddenly looked embarrassed. He had never actually explained how he came to be hanging from a Christmas tree.

'That's different,' he said. 'She woke me up.'

'But you called for help. You shouted, "Help! There's a wild goat in my room!"'

Mr Troll stared at his dad. 'You? Frighted by a little ninny goat?'

'Of course I wasn't frighted!' snapped Grumpa. 'I was trying to catch her!'

Ulrik frowned. 'You couldn't catch her climbing out the window, Grumpa.'

Grumpa opened his mouth, but for once he seemed to be lost for words.

Mr Troll burst out laughing. 'The fearless goat hunter!' he chuckled. 'Who's been telling fibwoppers now?'

The brave hunter sat down again. He suddenly looked smaller, like a balloon that had gone down.

'When did you last bags a goat, Dad?' asked Mr Troll. 'The truth.'

Grumpa's shoulders drooped. 'Not for years. The goats are so quick, I can't keep up with them.'

'But it's not just that, is it?' said Mrs Troll.

Grumpa shook his head sadly. 'It's the way they look when they're about to charge. Those sharp hornses. I suppose I just lost my nerve.'

Mr and Mrs Troll looked at each other. They hardly knew what to say. For years they had listened to Grumpa boasting about his skills as a hunter. He had claimed there wasn't a goat alive that he couldn't catch. Now it turned out his hunting days were over. Mrs Troll thought she understood why he spent so much time in his room. The truth was, a lot of things frightened him – not just goats but probably cars and noise and hairy-faced peeples.

Grumpa got to his feet. 'Don't worry, I'll pack my bag tonight,' he mumbled. 'I'll be gone before Trollmas.'

'Eggy – say something,' whispered Mrs Troll. But it was Ulrik who went over and gave his grumpa a hug.

'Don't go, Grumpa,' he said. 'It's all right to get frighted. I am sometimes.'

'Are you, Ulrik?'

'Yes, but do you know what I do?'

'What?'

'I give a big scaresome roar. GRARGHHHH!'

Grumpa laughed and put an arm round Ulrik. 'You know what?' he said. 'I think that roar *is* getting better.'

Happy Trollmas!

ULRIK SAT UP in bed. It felt like he'd been awake for hours but now at last he could see morning light through the curtains.

He wondered what Rosemary was doing on Trollmas Day. He was glad they had managed to smuggle her back to Longbottom Farm the previous night. She seemed pleased to see her mother. He imagined the farmer peeples' astonishment when he found his missing goat back in her pen.

Ulrik looked at his dad's rising-and-falling belly and jumped on top of him.

'WAKE UP, DAD! It's Trollmas Day!' he yelled.

'Uhhhh?' groaned Mr Troll.

'It's six o clock! Can we go downstairs? I want to open my presents!'

'All right, my ugglesome. Better see if Grumpa's awake.'

Five minutes later, Ulrik was bounding down the stairs. At the bottom he stopped and stared in wonder. Mr Troll had rescued the giant fir tree from the garden, minus its broken top. It now stood in the front room twinkling with lights. Socks hung from the branches, each of them stuffed with a present.

'Happy Trollmas, hairling!' beamed Mr and Mrs Troll.

Grumpa came down and they all watched Ulrik unwrap his presents. There was a mud painting kit from his mum and dad along with a storybook called *Goblinsocks and the Three Trolls**. From Grumpa there was something small and hard,

---

* *Trolls have their own trollish fairy tales in which they are always the hero. Favourite stories include* Trollerella, Tromplestiltskin *and* Sleeping Ugly.

wrapped in brown paper. Ulrik tore off the wrapping.

'A rock! Thanks, Grumpa! I'm collecting them.'

'This is a special one, Ulrik. It's my old rockball. I kept it for years, but now it's time I passed it on to you.'

'My own rockball!' said Ulrik, admiring it. 'Can we play a game?'

'Later on,' said Grumpa. 'I'll teach you a few tricks – the belly-butt and the ear-snapper.'

'Well,' said Mrs Troll. 'We'll all be needing some breakfast.'

'When are we going roaring, Dad?' asked Ulrik.

'As soon as it's dark,' promised Mr Troll. 'We'll start next door.'

Mrs Troll looked worried. 'Are you sure we should, Eggy? After what happened with the TV and the greenhouse, Mrs Priddle hasn't spoken to us.'

'This will cheer her up,' said Mr Troll confidently. 'There's nothing like a good roaring to put you in a gladful mood.'

Next door none of the Priddles was in a gladful

mood. Christmas Day with the Snorleys was proving every bit as dull as Mr Priddle had predicted.

'And this is Rainsworth Station,' said Mr Snorley, passing round another photo. 'It was rather foggy so you can't see it very well. That's Cynthia standing on Platform 5.'

Mr Priddle took the photo from his wife, trying not to yawn. It looked like the other one hundred photos of stations he had already seen. He glanced at his watch – only five o' clock. It might be hours before the Snorleys would be ready to go home.

Warren sat at the other end of the sofa from Alice Snorley – neither of them had spoken a word to each other since Alice had arrived.

'Well! Is it suppertime already?' asked Mr Priddle, breaking the silence.

His wife glared at him. 'Not for an hour, Roger. Perhaps we could play a party game.'

'Oh, we like games, don't we, Brian?' said Mrs Snorley. 'Brian's a marvel at quizzes. He has us in stitches.'

'Yes, I've got a terrific one about trains,' said Mr Snorley. 'Shall I pop home and get it?'

Mr Priddle groaned inwardly. Christmas Day and

they were doomed to answering questions about trains with the boring Snorleys! He wished something would happen – anything, really – the lights going out or the turkey exploding in the oven.

As if on cue a deafening noise made them all jump. It sounded like a thunderclap. Mrs Snorley ducked for cover behind her husband. Alice actually spoke – or at least squeaked.

'What was that?' asked Mr Snorley. 'It came from outside.'

'Don't go out there, Brian!' warned Mrs Snorley. 'It might be dangerous.'

Mr Snorley didn't look like he was about to go anywhere. He had turned very pale.

The rumble shook the house once again. The third time Mr Priddle knew where he'd heard it before. It was the same noise that woke him at seven o' clock every morning – only this time twice as loud. He went to the curtains and drew them back.

'Arghhh!' screamed Mrs Snorley as she caught sight of the four ugly faces grinning at them through the window.

'It's the Trolls,' said Mr Priddle. For once he sounded almost pleased.

'Don't let them in!' begged Mrs Snorley. 'They'll eat us!'

'Nonsense!' said Mr Priddle. 'They wouldn't hurt a fly.'

He opened the French windows and the trolls stepped in, dressed in their best clothes. Mr Troll was wearing his Trollmas jumper with a pattern of leaping goats. Mrs Troll had got a little carried away with her lipstick – the splodges on her cheeks made her look like a large, hairy doll. Grumpa was in his usual smelly goatskin coat, while Ulrik for some reason had a rock in his hand.

'Did you hear us roaring?' he asked.

'They could have heard you in Australia,' replied Mrs Priddle. 'You frightened the life out of us.'

Mr Troll seemed pleased. He explained that 'going roaring' was an old trollish custom.

'If we roar outside your cave three times it brings you good luck. Especially if you feed us.' His eyes strayed to the table set for supper.

'Oh well, you're welcome to join us for supper, aren't they, Jackie?' said Mr Priddle.

Mrs Priddle opened her mouth but seemed unable to speak.

'Marvellous,' said her husband. 'After all, it is Christmas. The more the merrier!'

The Trolls went round the room hugging and kissing everyone and wishing them 'Happy Trollmas'.

The Snorleys remained clinging to each other on the sofa, looking as if they might bolt for the door at any moment. Things were looking up, thought Mr Priddle.

An hour later dinner was served and the party began to warm up. Two bottles of wine were uncorked (the Trolls were not used to wine and it made them even more noisy than usual). They pulled crackers and wore paper hats lopsidedly on their heads. They ate second and third helpings of Mrs Priddle's roast turkey and declared it 'nearly as tastesome as goat pie' (even Ulrik forgot that he was a veggytellyum). After dessert Grumpa stood on the table to sing an old trollish hunting song and no one seemed to mind when he put his foot in the trifle.

'A game!' cried Mrs Priddle when the song ended. 'We were going to play a game!'

'Shall I pop home and fetch my quiz?' offered Mr Snorley.

'No!' chorused the Priddles loudly and all at once.

'I got a game for Trollmas,' said Ulrik. 'It's called Rockball.'

'Rockball?' said Mrs Snorley. 'I don't think I've ever heard of it.'

'It's great,' said Ulrik. 'This is the rock.' He passed a rock about the size of a small cannonball across the table for Mrs Snorley to admire.

'You've got the ball so you can start,' said Grumpa.

'Oh! Me? What am I meant to do with it?' asked Mrs Snorley.

'Try and keep it,' said Ulrik.

'How do I do that?'

'Run!' advised Grumpa.

'Run?' said Mrs Snorley. 'Run where?'

'Anywheres,' said Mr Troll. 'Before we grab you by the legses and snaffle it off you.'

Mrs Snorley saw that Ulrik and Mr Troll were already getting to their feet. She screamed and fled from the table, holding the rock out in front of her as if it was a time bomb.

The Trolls chased her through the kitchen and out into the back garden, pursued by Alice, Warren and a worried Mr Snorley. Grumpa and Mrs Troll stood with the Priddles by the back door to watch them go.

'I do hope they're not going to get carried away,' said Mrs Priddle.

From somewhere in the darkness came a surprised scream closely followed by a roar of triumph.

'It sounds like Mrs Snorley's the one being carried away,' grinned Grumpa.

It had turned out to be quite a merry Trollmas after all.